# AN EVENING WITH THADDEUS

- -

A two-act drama

by
**John Glass**

**john@studentplays.org**

## <u>Copyright information. Please read!</u>

# ☞ About Student Plays ☜

Student Plays consists of **John Glass, Jackie Jernigan,** and **Dominic Torres**. We are a group of playwrights and directors that have written scripts for middle school, high school, and the university. We are proud of the variety of ages that our scripts serve, and we are particularly proud of our *Latino-themed plays*. These are scripts that focus on Latino youth and the Latino experience. Any school can perform a Latino-themed play: it just requires a general introduction and exposure to the Spanish language, something that most schools and students already have.

To learn more, or to communicate with one of the playwrights, contact us at john@studentplays.org.

**"An Evening with Thaddeus"** is one of the few 'adult plays' within *Student Plays*.

# <u>List of Characters</u>

**COURTNEY**       Early thirties. Aggressive.
Ambitious. Quick-witted.

**SHAI**       Late twenties, brother of
Courtney. Kind and simple.

**JOEL**       Fifties. Man of absolutely
few words. Simple, very slow
in speech and movement.
Wears a pair of gloves
throughout entire play.

**GRANDPA**       Seventies or early eighties.
Crotchety, sarcastic. Is able to
walk a little but uses a
wheelchair.

The entire play takes place in an old antebellum
home in Galveston, Texas. The house is located in
one of the back bay/inlet areas of the Gulf Coast.
The time is a weekday in the late spring of 2002. A
hurricane has been projected to hit land that
evening.

Throughout the play, there is the sound of strong blasts of wind and the occasional banging of wood against the outside windows of the house. These sounds progress as the play moves forward. There is also the repeated sound of broken glass late in **ACT TWO.**

All of **ACT ONE** takes place in the same set, the living room and dining room of the house. There are several windows throughout the set, and scattered pieces of plywood.

All three scenes of **ACT TWO** are in different bedrooms, but each room is extremely similar. The rooms are unused bedrooms in the house, each having a basic setup of chairs and a table.

☛ **General Requirements:** Flashlights, hammers, rain ponchos, two cordless drills, boxes of screws and nails, an old lantern, candles, a small radio, various sizes of scrap wood (very thin plywood/paneling) and GRANDPA's box, which is a small cardboard box containing papers and journals. The box should be thin and portable, and not too heavy or bulky. A wheelchair.

\*\*  **Set Notes:**  During the play, the "drilling of the plywood" over the windows can be a simple task. Thin pieces of trim can be drilled to the walls of the set to depict a window, and then the actors can drill pieces of scrap plywood *into the trim.* This may be better than drilling plywood all over the walls of the set. The "pieces of plywood" in the play can be <u>small, very thin</u> pieces of paneling, or any other kind of light wood.

# ACT ONE
## <u>Scene One</u>

At RISE: *The kitchen and dining room of the house. Morning. COURTNEY is working with a drill, screwing pieces of plywood to the windows. After a few seconds, enter SHAI.*

**COURTNEY**  There you are.

**SHAI**  Hey. Yeah, I'm back.

**COURTNEY**  About time.

**SHAI**  Um. Thaddeus? Is that what they're really calling this one?

**COURTNEY**  Well. We had Pablo, Robert, Steven . . . and now it's Thaddeus.

**SHAI**  The names they come up with. Someone's getting paid to do all that.

**COURTNEY**  Yeah. Shai, where have you been? I've been working all morning.

**SHAI**  Trying to track Vicki down. I think she's panicking like everyone else.

**COURTNEY**  Well. They're projecting this one to be huge.

**SHAI**  Please . . . it's just gonna blow over. Like always.

**COURTNEY**  There's supposed to be an evacuation.

**SHAI**  I heard. Can they do that?

**COURTNEY**  I don't know. Never really had a serious storm before.
>    *(Pause)*
Can you help me?

>    *(He slowly picks up a drill, begins to help.)*

**SHAI**  Did the neighbors leave?

**COURTNEY**  Yeah.  Their cars are all gone.

>    *(Pause as they work.)*

**COURTNEY**  I needed you earlier. We might need more supplies.

**SHAI**  I was trying to get ahold of Vicki. I went over to her house, left, then went back again. Waited around. I think she may have gone to Dallas.

**COURTNEY**  To her aunt's?

**SHAI**  Yeah. I think so.
        *(Pause.)*
Guess who called while I was driving home?

**COURTNEY**  Who?

**SHAI**  Grandpa.

**COURTNEY**  Grandpa? He has your cell number?

**SHAI**  I gave it to him the last time we saw him. He wants to come over.

**COURTNEY**  Over *here*?

**SHAI**  Mhmm. He said he was concerned about us.

**COURTNEY**  Concerned. Whatever. He *needs* us.

**SHAI** Yeah. I think so. He sounded urgent.

**COURTNEY** I don't want that know-it-all over here. Him and his warped, outdated views on everything. That panel was a train wreck.

**SHAI** Well. It wasn't ideal.

**COURTNEY** Don't be naive about Grandpa. And you know that Mom wouldn't want him here either. Not that I'm worrying about her opinion.

**SHAI** Still . . . we can't just *leave* him there can we? That area floods easily . . .

**COURTNEY** You've been doubting this storm is coming. Now you seem pretty sure it's headed our way.

**SHAI** No. My mind's just all over the place. I'm worried about him. And about Vicki.

**SHAI** They're family. They need to be here. *(Beat. Puts the drill down.)* Good God, Courtney, what's wrong with us? Here we are, in this huge house, in the middle of a potential hurricane. And it's just you and me.

**COURTNEY**  Ha. What else did you *expect?*

**SHAI**  In the old days, sheesh, families hunkered down together without even thinking about it. They just did it. Stuck together. But now . . . *(Beat )* What about Russell?

**COURTNEY**  Don't know. We've played phone tag all morning. That's why I haven't gotten more done here.

**SHAI**  See, that's what I mean, right there. *He* should be here too. He's more or less family. *(Beat. Slowly begins to exit.)* Look, this is bothering me. I'll be back. I'm going to drop by Vicki's one more time.

**COURTNEY**  You just left there!

**SHAI**  I know. But she may have returned. Maybe I can catch her before they leave.

**COURTNEY**  You sure about that? You know how you get . . .

**SHAI**  Nothing like that is going to happen. And I really want to see Marshall.

**COURTNEY** Lord . . .

> *(Pause.)*

Well. Are you going to get Grandpa?

**SHAI** I thought you didn't want him over here.

**COURTNEY** Well, I don't. But we might feel horrible if we didn't at least try. *(Beat.)* Or—or, wait, ughh, it's *Grandpa*. What am I saying?

**SHAI** I'll go get him. He should be here with us.

**COURTNEY** Okay. Well, go then. If you must. But hurry. It's almost noon. The weather's getting worse.

**SHAI** I know.

**COURTNEY** We might need extra batteries. And maybe candles. And I'll need your help.

**SHAI** Okay. I'll be back.

**COURTNEY** Hey . . .

**SHAI** What?

**COURTNEY**  Be careful.

> *(He nods and exits. Long pause as she*
> *works, periodically checking her phone. A*
> *blast of wind opens the door up. JOEL*
> *slowly enters the doorframe and stands*
> *there quietly. He is wearing old coveralls,*
> *gloves, and boots, with a hammer stuck in*
> *his belt loop. He is wet from the rain. In the*
> *next few minutes, there is the gradual sound*
> *of howling wind and of wood banging*
> *against wood.)*

**COURTNEY**  Uh, hello? Can I help you?

**JOEL**  Hello.

**COURTNEY**  Oh . . . *Joel?* Is that you?

**JOEL**  How's everything?

**COURTNEY**  Well, uh, how are *you*?

**JOEL**  Good.

**COURTNEY**  Come in, come in. Oh. You need a towel, hang on. *(Walks over to retrieve one.)* Wow, what are you doing here?

**JOEL**  Sorry. Thought maybe ya'll could use a hand out there.

**COURTNEY**  Where?

**JOEL**  With the windows. Boarding them up.

**COURTNEY**  Oh. Yeah. There's a bunch of windows. God, *too many* windows. *(Hands him the towel.)* There you go. So, wow. I haven't seen you in years. *Uncle* Joel, right?
*(A nervous laugh)* We never knew what to call you.

**JOEL**  Sorry. This is probably weird.

**COURTNEY**  No, not at all.

**JOEL**  I just . . . well, the storm is coming. And I was out driving around.

**COURTNEY**  Uh, right. It's definitely coming. It's hurricane season, right? You didn't have a place to go?

**JOEL**  Not really. No.

**COURTNEY**  Oh . . . okay. Well.

**JOEL**  Some of your loose wood is out there, banging again the side of the house. Thought maybe I could fix it.

**COURTNEY**  Oh, good. You brought that hammer?

**JOEL**  Yes, I did. I have tools in my car.

**COURTNEY**  Oh. Why?

**JOEL**  I use them.

**COURTNEY**  Okay. Great. *(Beat.)* So where are you living? I haven't seen you since . . . well, I can't remember when.

**JOEL**  I was out in New Mexico.

**COURTNEY**  Oh. Is my dad still out there?

**JOEL**  Yes. Yes, he is. You don't mind if I stay here? Tonight?

**COURTNEY** No. Um. That's fine.

**JOEL** Good.

**COURTNEY** Yeah, it's no problem. You . . . you *are* family.

**JOEL** Right.

**COURTNEY** You want to take your gloves off? You want—

**JOEL** Could I have another towel?

**COURTNEY** Yes, of course. *(She goes to get one.)* Of course. We have plenty.

**JOEL** I appreciate it. I got all wet.

**COURTNEY** You *did* get all wet.

**JOEL** I was outside for a while. Over on this side. *(Pointing)* Looking at the loose wood.

**COURTNEY** Um. Okay. Here you go. *(Beat. She notices her phone on the table.)*

Oh, hang on. I missed this call. Hang on one sec, Joel. *(She plays with her phone for a few seconds, aggravated, then puts it down, hard.)* Dammit.

**JOEL**  Where's your mother?

**COURTNEY**  She's not here. She's in the Middle East. Shai and I live here now.

**JOEL**  I think I saw him leaving. When I was outside.

**COURTNEY**  Yeah. We moved in here about a year ago. Mom basically gave the house to us.

**JOEL**  Gave it to you?

**COURTNEY**  Well. Shai and I were living somewhere else at the time, and then . . . well, we needed somewhere new to live. Mom was moving out of the country so she just let us have it.

**JOEL**  I didn't know.

**COURTNEY**  Sort of a long story.

**JOEL**  It usually is.

**COURTNEY** Huh?

**JOEL** In this family, it usually is a long story. *(She gradually picks up the drill, returns to work.)*

**COURTNEY** Right. Um. So you're back in Galveston. Where are you living?

**JOEL** In a mobile home.

**COURTNEY** Oh.

**JOEL** Over in Navco. The Windpipers.

**COURTNEY** Yes, I know where those are.

**JOEL** Thing's gonna be toast. All this wind and rain.

**COURTNEY** Oh. Okay.

**JOEL** Sorry. I know I'm intruding.

**COURTNEY** No, it's fine, Joel. Really.

**JOEL** I was out, driving around. I remember that your mom lived here . . .

**COURTNEY**  Yep.

**JOEL**  Came by and saw the lights on. Decided I'd knock.

**COURTNEY**  It's fine. Seriously. Hang on, I'm getting another call.

**COURTNEY** *(Picks it up, pushes buttons, becomes angry.)* Damn! His calls keep dropping! And this reception is nearly gone. *(She slams phone down on table, picks up the drill.)* Sorry. I'm waiting to hear from somebody. Hey, um. I kind of need to get back to work, Joel. I've got to find more screws and— *(He stops her, holds her arm)*

**JOEL**  I want to thank you. I just need a place to stay.

**COURTNEY**  Yeah. Of course. Don't worry about it.

**JOEL**  You won't even know I'm here.

**COURTNEY**  Right.

**JOEL**  Thank you so much.

**COURTNEY**  Don't even think about it. It's not a problem. Make yourself at home, Joel.

**JOEL**  I can cover those windows on the outside. On the side facing the pier.

**COURTNEY**  Gosh, I forgot about those. Shit, this house is huge. Okay, thanks. Shai's drill is here, somewhere.

**JOEL**  I have my hammer. *(Begins to exit.)*

**COURTNEY**  Okay. And Joel? There's an old clothesline attached to one of the windowsills. It's kind of in the way. It's really thick. I was trying to cut it with a utility knife. The knife is out there – you'll see it.

**JOEL**  A knife?

**COURTNEY**  Yeah. On the windowsill.

**JOEL**  Okay. A knife.

**COURTNEY**  But be careful. It's old. You can't close it – the blade is always out, and it's really sharp.

**JOEL**  I can take care of myself.

**COURTNEY**  I'm only saying, you know, be careful with it. It's a large knife, and the blade—

**JOEL**  I told you. I can take care of myself. *(Pause as he stares at her)*

**COURTNEY**  Okay.

**JOEL**  Believe me. I've always taken care of myself. *(He exits. COURTNEY stares at the door for a moment, and exits. Lights fade.)*

# ACT ONE
## Scene Two

At RISE:   *The same day, a little later in the afternoon. SHAI is screwing plywood to the kitchen windows. GRANDPA is eating a snack. On a table are screws, a few small bags, candles, a small jump drive, a few rain ponchos, and GRANDPA's box. Small pieces of plywood are scattered throughout the room. The wind lightly howls as the scene opens.*

**SHAI**  Where is it? In your bathroom?

**GRANDPA**  Yeah. Dammit. Sorry.

**SHAI**  It's okay. I can go back and get it for you.

**GRANDPA**  Can you?

**SHAI**  Yes. Let me finish a little more work in here.

**GRANDPA**  Okay.

**SHAI**  Can I grab that, uh, box of old comic books too?

**GRANDPA**  The funny books?

**SHAI**  Yes.

**GRANDPA**  Sure. Why not?

**SHAI**  I collect comics, you know.

**GRANDPA**  Yeah, I remember. You told me.

**SHAI**  Is there anything else there?

**GRANDPA**  Nah. I've got a change-of-clothes. My wallet. I've got my strongbox. *(Pats it.)* Right here.

**SHAI**  Okay.

**GRANDPA**  I'll just need my medicine. I'm okay right now.

**SHAI**  All right. I'll go get it. *(He looks down at the mess on the table.)* Grandpa, can you help me move this stuff out of the way? I need some room.

**GRANDPA**  Sure.

**SHAI** Thanks.

> *(Pause. They slide everything down to the end of the table. SHAI places extra screws and drill bits on the table as GRANDPA winds up holding a handful of newspaper and the jump drive, and he simply stuffs them in the side pocket of his chair. SHAI resumes his work, screwing the plywood to the windows.)*

**SHAI** There we go. Good, thanks.

**GRANDPA** Yep.

**SHAI** Much better. More room.

**GRANDPA** I'll just put whatever this crap is in here, in my chair.

**SHAI** Grandpa, there's other crackers in the pantry, if you want more.

**GRANDPA** I'm okay. I'm fine. *(Beat. Looks around.)* Well. Tell you what. Doesn't look like your mom ever did a lot with the old place.

**SHAI** Yeah. Well, me and Court have done a little work. Put new tile in the bathrooms. Painted the hallways. Lot left to do, though.

**GRANDPA** I can tell.

**SHAI** The outside of the house is the worst. Lots of woodwork to do. That old siding. There are a million windows out there.

**GRANDPA** Oh yeah.

**SHAI** Oh, Grandpa, we also have some juice.

**GRANDPA** I told you I was all right. You didn't hear me?

**SHAI** Oh. Right. Sorry.

**GRANDPA** Where did you say your sister was?

**SHAI** At the other end of the house, I think. Working on the windows.

**GRANDPA** Hmm. Yeah, I got a few memories around here. Weird how Ruby just up and left. Or whatever she did. Why did you and Courtney move back here?

**SHAI** It was . . . it was a weird time.

**GRANDPA** What do you mean?

(Pause.)

**SHAI** Well. Vicki and I broke up. She's my wife, you know. We're not divorced, just separated. And then Courtney was going through her own drama.

**GRANDPA** Her what?

**SHAI** Her drama. She was dealing with her own relationship. Or rather the *break-up* of her relationship.

**GRANDPA** She and that guy split up?

**SHAI** Yep. And Mom was really getting involved with her political stuff. You know how Mom is.

**GRANDPA** Oh yeah. Doesn't surprise me. Like mother, like daughter.

*(Enter COURTNEY, holding her phone and her drill. Unseen by GRANDPA, she stands for a minute, watching them talk. From this point on, GRANDPA begins to gradually cough, more and more throughout the rest of the act.)*

**SHAI**  She met this guy, this Palestinian dude. And *bam*, now she's living in the Middle East. She basically just let us have the house. So here we are. It all just, like, happened at the same time. Mom was barely living here anyway.

**GRANDPA**  Goodness. The Middle East. What's she doing over there? Learning how to hijack American airplanes?

**COURTNEY**  Palestinians don't do that.

**GRANDPA**  Huh? *(Turns to face her)* Well, well . . .

**COURTNEY**  And if they do, it's because our ridiculous foreign policy drove them to do it. Hello, Grandpa. *(She walks over to them, puts phone and drill down on table.)*

**GRANDPA**  Well, howdy, howdy.

**COURTNEY**  It's, um, good to have you here.

**GRANDPA**  It's good to be here. How you doin'?

**COURTNEY**  Doing well. *(Quickly turning to SHAI)* Okay, look, we need to get the other batteries. Where are they?

**SHAI**  I told you, in the closet.

**COURTNEY**  I checked in there. Didn't see them.

**SHAI**  They're in there. In the big hallway closet. Very top shelf.

**COURTNEY**  Can you get them?

**SHAI**  Weren't you just in there?

**COURTNEY**  Shai, just get them, please! I can't reach that high.

**SHAI**  Okay. Damn, Courtney. *(Begins to exit.)*

**COURTNEY**  Come on. I'm not as tall as you.

**SHAI** I know, hang on.

> (*He exits. For the next few minutes,*
> *COURTNEY assesses the table in front of*
> *her, inspecting her drill bits and drill, etc.*
> *Going forward, as GRANDPA talks, he*
> *gradually rolls his chair over to far stage*
> *right or stage left, absentmindedly.*)

**COURTNEY** Okay. I want to be sure I have enough drill bits and screws. And I've got to find my jump drive. I put it down in here, somewhere. *(Notices the box.)* What is that box? That yours?

**GRANDPA** Yes.

**COURTNEY** What is it?

**GRANDPA** It's just my personal box. Taxes, social security stuff. My journals. You know.

**COURTNEY** Oh.

**GRANDPA** That's all.

**COURTNEY** Hmmpph.

*(Pause. She remains occupied with the table.)*

**GRANDPA**  Well, shoot. How are things?

**COURTNEY**  Good. Everything is good, I guess.

**GRANDPA**  You aren't defending the Palestinians now, are you?

**COURTNEY**  I beg your pardon?

**GRANDPA**  Well, last time I saw you, you, um . . . you had all this liberal guilt. How the white male race has been destructive throughout history or something. Remember? And just now, you made a comment about the Palestinians. So . . . *(Her phone buzzes. She is disgusted as she picks it up and listens.)*

**GRANDPA**  . . . you sounded like maybe you were defending them.

**COURTNEY**  Russell? Hello?? I can hardly hear you. Russell?
        *(Pause)*

Are you coming over here? What? I can't hear you!!
*(She plays with phone, then slams it down on
counter. A whistle of wind is heard, along with the
loud banging of wood. She returns her attention to
GRANDPA.)*

**COURTNEY** Listen to me, Grandpa. And listen
good.

**GRANDPA** I'm listening.

**COURTNEY** We're not gonna do this this time.
No arguing over politics. Over history. This is *my*
house.

**GRANDPA** What in hell is that banging noise?

**COURTNEY** And you play by *my* rules here! Got
it?

**GRANDPA** What *is* that?

**COURTNEY** Okay??

**GRANDPA** Hang on, that sound is coming from
right out here. Wha . . .?? *(Enter JOEL, who steps
right out in front of GRANDPA, holding hammer.)*

Oh. Uh, someone's here, Courtney. *(Recognizes JOEL and screams. Backs his chair up furiously.)* HEY! IT'S . . . YOU! Hey, keep back!

**COURTNEY** Oh, shit.

**JOEL** I need more nails.

**GRANDPA** I didn't know anybody else was here! *(Enter SHAI, holding a bag of batteries)*

**COURTNEY** Grandpa, stop. Nothing's going to happen.

**GRANDPA** What in the hell!?

**JOEL** I need some more nails.

**GRANDPA** Keep this three-fingered juvenile away from me!

**SHAI** Uncle Joel?

**JOEL** Watch your mouth, old man. I haven't said a word to you.

**GRANDPA** That don't make a difference! My memory is like a steel trap, boy! You keep your distance!

**SHAI** Courtney, what's going on here?

**COURTNEY** Damn, damn, damn . . .

**GRANDPA** You're damn right, *damn, damn, damn*!

**COURTNEY** I forgot. I totally forgot.

**SHAI** Courtney, what is it?

**COURTNEY** I didn't even think about it. He's . . . *(Beat.)* Shai, Uncle Joel's back in town. He showed up when you were gone.

**JOEL** I can leave.

**COURTNEY** Where would you go, Joel? The weather is getting ludicrous out there!

**GRANDPA** It wouldn't hurt my feelings none.

**JOEL** You need to shut your trap, Pops.

**COURTNEY** JOEL! Stop!

**SHAI** *(Slowly remembering)* Oh. Yeah . . .

**GRANDPA** Your uncle here and I cut grass together one summer, sonny.

**SHAI** Okay . . .

**GRANDPA** Damnedest thing, of all people. *Us* working together.

**COURTNEY** We don't have to go into this now, do we?

**GRANDPA** Sonny here had a little, uh, accident.

**JOEL** It didn't *have* to happen.

**COURTNEY** This has to end! Seriously! ALL OF THAT WAS AGES AGO!

> *(Pause. Everybody is stunned at how she controls the moment.)*

**COURTNEY**  Now, LOOK! If we are going to stay in this house together, then we *have* to make this work! OKAY??

**GRANDPA**  All right.

**COURTNEY**  We have no choice here!

**JOEL**  Hmpph.

**GRANDPA**  I'll behave.

**SHAI**  *(Extending hand to JOEL)* How are you? Are you back in town?

**JOEL**  Yes. Been back for a while.

**SHAI**  Well, good. It's great to see you. It's been forever.

**COURTNEY**  And Grandpa, I was serious a minute ago! You play by *our* rules here!

**GRANDPA**  Okay, okay, okay . . .

**COURTNEY**  No arguing about the Palestinians. Or the Native Americans.

**GRANDPA** *Who?*

**COURTNEY** Or *anybody*. Are you going to be able to behave yourself?

**GRANDPA** Just what am I? A ten-year-old? *(Pointing to JOEL.)* It's *him* that I'm worried about!

**JOEL** I'm warning you, Pops.

**GRANDPA** See what I mean! He loves making those threats!

**SHAI** Well, Grandpa, look, you stay over here, for now. *(He begins to push the wheelchair farther away from JOEL.) Okay?*

**GRANDPA**. Keep rolling, sonny.

**SHAI** And Uncle Joel can stay over there. Right? Or anywhere but near Grandpa.

**COURTNEY** Right.

**SHAI** I mean, it's a big house. There's tons of room.

**COURTNEY** Let's get moving, ya'll. We have a lot of work left. There are five bedrooms in this damn house, which means a ton of damn windows. And then there's also the outside windows. We don't have time for any nonsense!

**JOEL** I just came inside to get some nails. *(Picks up a box from table.)* Um. Somebody was here earlier. The civil service or somebody.

**COURTNEY** The civil service?

**JOEL** That's what their truck said.

**COURTNEY** They actually came? For the evacuation?

**JOEL** I guess. Said we had to leave. I told them we weren't leaving.

**SHAI** You told them that?

**JOEL** I told them. They said okay. Didn't look like they wanted to stick around.

**SHAI** Wow . . .

**COURTNEY** Well. I'm not going anywhere. It'll be fine.

**SHAI** Uncle Joel, come on, I'll help you outside.

**JOEL** Okay. *(SHAI grabs a poncho and his drill. They begin to exit.)*

**SHAI** Is that your car over at the neighbor's?

**JOEL** Yes. Looked like it might be safe there.

**SHAI** Might be okay.

**GRANDPA** Shouldn't he be using screws out there? With a drill? And not nails??

**JOEL** I'll do this the way I want.

**COURTNEY** It's fine, it's fine. Just *go*, Joel, please.

**SHAI** Yeah, come on.

**COURTNEY** You guys go. Ignore him.

*(They exit. Pause. COURTNEY begins working in this room. GRANDPA is disgusted.)*

**GRANDPA**  I can't believe what I've gotten into. Of all people, your uncle Joel!

**COURTNEY**  It'll be *okay*, Grandpa.

**GRANDPA**  If you say so.

**COURTNEY**  Relax.

**GRANDPA**  Hmmph. Easier said than done.

*(Long pause. GRANDPA stares at COURTNEY as she works.)*

**GRANDPA**  So . . . you didn't graduate?

**COURTNEY**  I've got a little over a year left. I told you that at that academic panel. At the university.

**GRANDPA**  Damnation. Probably forgot. Yeah. That panel.

**COURTNEY**  Yes, that panel. You made me look like a fool up there. You caused a real scene, I hope you know.

**GRANDPA**  Well, all you did was go on and on about how white men are the downfall of all humanity.

**COURTNEY**  Sorry if the truth hurts.

**GRANDPA**  It's only true because, historically, they've basically been the main ones in power. That's just mathematics, hon. I told you.

**COURTNEY**  So you're saying that it's fair, then? Is that what you're saying?

**GRANDPA**  Whether it's fair or not is for a whole different discussion. Geez, I can't believe this. Are you getting your masters degree in this anti-male business?

**COURTNEY**  I'm getting my *PhD,* Grandpa. I told you that too. That was only six months ago. And they don't offer degrees in *anti-male business.*

**GRANDPA** Your PhD. Wow. Well, damn. Congratulations. That's impressive.

**COURTNEY** Thank you.

**GRANDPA** I remember now. I know you were looking for a teaching job. Or were *going* to be looking for a teaching job.

**COURTNEY** I still am. *(Stops working, looks through bag on the table.)* I don't believe these are the only batteries we have.

**GRANDPA** You, uh, you on the skids with your boyfriend?

**COURTNEY** What? Is there anything Shai *didn't* tell you?

**GRANDPA** He just said that things didn't work out, and that's why you moved back here.

**COURTNEY** I don't see why that was important to bring up. *(Beat. She stops searching and suddenly looks around.)* Wait. I have *got* to find my jump drive. Where did I put it?? It was right on this table!

**GRANDPA**  Well at least you two didn't get married.

**COURTNEY**  *(Still occupied with looking.)* Sheesh. Oh, please. I almost made that mistake. I don't plan on *ever* getting married. *Or* having kids.

**GRANDPA**  You know what the divorce rate is nowadays? Time was, people were frightened of getting divorced. Marriage meant something. But nowadays, shoot . . young folks are running to the courthouse to split up. Especially—well . . .

**COURTNEY**  Especially *what?*

**GRANDPA**  Well, especially black people. They don't stay married. Hell, they don't even *get* married.

**COURTNEY**  I beg your pardon? *Black* people? You mean *African Americans?*

**GRANDPA**  You know who I mean.

**COURTNEY**  How do you know they don't marry?

**GRANDPA** Look, don't get your panties in a wad. I'm only—

**COURTNEY** I'll get my panties in a wad if I want. It's my house! Watch what you say around here!

**GRANDPA** All I'm saying is that they don't marry!

**COURTNEY** Grandpa, my fiancée was black. *Is* black.

**GRANDPA** Well . . . which is it?

**COURTNEY** *Was*. We broke up. He's the one that I'm sure Shai told you about.

**GRANDPA** Oh. Actually, yes, he did . . . *(Pause as GRANDPA starts to gradually coughs. COURTNEY picks up phone again and pushes buttons)*

**GRANDPA** All I'm trying to say is that . . . maybe it's better that you *didn't* get married. Maybe . . . well, maybe you can *do* better.

**COURTNEY** Huh?

**GRANDPA**  You don't need to be marrying a guy like that. You're better off without him. Hell, I served with 'em in the army. I should know.

**COURTNEY**  I don't believe this! Mom's always told us that you were like this. But I can't believe what I'm hearing!

**GRANDPA**  What did I say??

**COURTNEY**  Grandpa, just drop everything! *(Slams phone down.)* There's no time to discuss my boyfriend with you. I wish he were here to defend himself! Anyway, there is work to do. That hurricane is gonna be here soon!

**GRANDPA**  Your *ex*.

**COURTNEY**  What?

**GRANDPA**  Your *ex-boyfriend*. You just said *boyfriend*.

> *(Pause as they stare at each other. She picks up drill, begins to exit, points it right at him.)*

**COURTNEY**  Do me a favor. Keep your opinions to yourself.

**GRANDPA**  Wait. Where are you going?

**COURTNEY**  To the other bedrooms. There's work to be done.

**GRANDPA**  Don't leave me in here alone! I'm still your grandfather, you know!

**COURTNEY**  Would you relax? Uncle Joel's outside. And besides, he's harmless.

**GRANDPA**  Harmless, my foot.

**COURTNEY**  Nothing's going to happen. I'll just be back here.

**GRANDPA**  Do you know what happened between us? *(Begins to coughs again, this time worse.)*

**COURTNEY**  Of course I know what happened. I know all about it.

**GRANDPA**  It was ridiculous! But he blamed *me* for it . . . *(Coughs horribly.)*

**COURTNEY** Grandpa . . . ? Ughhhh!
*(Pause. She stares at him.)*
Are you okay? Do you need water?

**GRANDPA** No. I need my medicine.
*(Pause)*
I didn't bring it. Shai is supposed to go get it for me.

**COURTNEY** Ohh . . ! (Calls out.) SHAI? SHAI?
*(Pause.)*
Oh, what am I doing? He can't hear me in all that
wind and rain. Grandpa, you don't have *any* here
with you? *(Walks over to the door)*

**GRANDPA** No.

**COURTNEY** Uggh!! This is the last thing we
need. How could you not bring it??

**GRANDPA** I dunno. We were in a hurry.

**COURTNEY** SHAI!!!
*(Pause.)*
I can't believe this. *(Enter SHAI, suddenly.)*

**COURTNEY** There you are.

**SHAI** What's up?

**COURTNEY** Shai, go get Grandpa's medicine.

**SHAI** Oh, damn! His medicine!

**GRANDPA** I need it, sonny.

**SHAI** Going now. I still have your keys.

**GRANDPA** It's sitting right on top of the bathroom sink. It's a little pink bottle. You'll see it.

**SHAI** Alright. Hey, what about your comic books?

**GRANDPA** Go ahead. They're in the living room. On top of my old Magnavox record player in the corner. In an old wooden box.

**SHAI** Okay. Wooden box. Got it.

**GRANDPA** On top of the Magnavox. And don't forget the medicine, sonny. It's a little pink bottle.

**SHAI** Bathroom sink. Okay. *(Begins to exit.)*

**COURTNEY** Shai, go! The police might be out soon, enforcing the evacuation! And I need your help here! *(Quickly picks up her phone, studies it.)*

**SHAI** I'm going, I'm going! *(He exits in a hurry.)*

**COURTNEY** Comic books! Stupid . . .!

**GRANDPA** He's not taking you-know-who with him, is he?

**COURTNEY** I don't know. But he better not waste time by going to check on his so-called *family* again. They're not worried about him so why should he even bother?

**GRANDPA** Who are you talking about? Oh, his step-son?

**COURTNEY** Something like that. If you ask him, it's his *son*.

**GRANDPA** Hmmm.
    *(Pause.)*
His son, huh? Well. Thank God it's not his actual son. He shouldn't breeding with something like that. He was married to that witch, wasn't he?

**COURTNEY** *(Completely preoccupied with phone)*
Yeah. Um, yes, Grandpa. She actually *is* a witch. Or
at least she claims to be.

**GRANDPA** A witch. What the hell is this world
coming to? *(Beat. He watches her.)* I don't
understand those cellular gadgets. Who are you
communicating with? You haven't put that thing
down since I've been here.

**COURTNEY** Nobody. It's nobody. My phone is
all messed up. I can't send any messages but I can
receive them. There's someone that I thought might
need a place to stay. *(Flings phone down, picks up
the drill.)* Screw this. I don't know why I'm so
concerned with him. I've gotta finish these
windows.

> *(Pause. She works, and basically tunes
> GRANDPA out. The sound of thunder and
> wind is heard. Grandpa gradually coughs
> off and on, throughout the rest of the scene.)*

**GRANDPA** Mmmm. Listen to that wind and rain.
Oh, the storms like this that I've seen. Hurricane
Bobby. Hurricane Emily. Hurricane Camille, back
in 1969. That one was a doozy. Joann and I were in

Louisiana then. Bunkered down in that little house . . . *(He laughs as he reflects)* Yeah. Lots of storms. There was a storm just like this. An old house . . . a night exactly like this in Germany.

*(Pause. He gazes off, deep in thought)*

We saw some crazy things back then. Oh, man.

*(Pause.)*

Me and a few soldiers from the 97th came across this farmhouse. We went inside to get out of the weather. Horrible storm! Just horrible! We went inside . . . and there were some sounds coming from the loft. They were up there . . . yep. Making all that noise.

*(Pause.)*

Yep. A night just like this . . .

*(Beat. He looks at COURTNEY.)*

Well, I wanna hear about your schooling. You're still doing history, right?

**COURTNEY** Uh, yeah. Isn't that obvious?

**GRANDPA** I want to talk to you about that. Maybe try and help you.

**COURTNEY** Huh?

**GRANDPA** Remember: I'm old. I've *lived* history. I told you about the 97th Infantry, right?

**COURTNEY** Yes, I know you were in the war. You were just talking about it. We aren't *that* distant, Grandpa.

**GRANDPA** What's your big paper on? Your, uh, your—

**COURTNEY** My dissertation.

**GRANDPA**. Right.

**COURTNEY** I've told you before. I feel like it's a mistake to bring it up. But it's on the Tuskegee Airmen.

**GRANDPA** Oh. Right. The Tuskegee Airmen. Sorry, I forget things. I was thinking it might be on the Middle East.

**COURTNEY** No.

**GRANDPA** Thought maybe you were writing about how *evil* Israel is. How *glorified* Palestine is. *(Scoffs.)* Palestine. What the hell got into your mother and caused her to move over there? Palestine, of all places. Lord.

**COURTNEY**. What's wrong with Palestine?

**GRANDPA** Nothing's wrong with Palestine. But Ruby's got no business over there, trying to save everybody. Or whatever she's doing. Those people will dismiss her just as they dismiss anybody else that's not one of their kind.
*(Pause)*
But then, Courtney, look at you. You've got your education and everything. You've done all right.

**COURTNEY** Well . . . *(With great reluctance.)* Thank you. I'm trying.

**GRANDPA** You really have. You want to teach at a college, right?

**COURTNEY** That's the plan. I'm in the process of applying right now. It's a cutthroat business, especially for female professors, trying to break in.

**GRANDPA** Latest stats I read say that the number of new female professors across the country has increased.

**COURTNEY**  Whatever. Does that make you feel better?

**GRANDPA**  I didn't give a damn to begin with. But seriously, maybe I can help you.

**COURTNEY**  How can you help me? You keep saying that.

**GRANDPA**  Well, I made a few calls a while back. You never know where it might go.

**COURTNEY**  You *what*?

**GRANDPA**  I made some calls for you. But first, tell me: what kind of teaching you gonna be doing?

**COURTNEY**  Who did you call??

**GRANDPA**  You're not gonna be doing any of that *revisionist* crap, are you?

**COURTNEY**  Excuse me?

**GRANDPA**  Revisionist history. Where everything is re-written to appease the liberals. And the whiney-asses. You know. We talked about this before at that panel thing.

**COURTNEY** No, *you* talked about this. You stood up and caused a big scene. *(Stops working and puts head in her hands, agitated)* I was hoping we wouldn't get around to this. Oh, Grandpa, why is it always *something* with you? Why are things never just easy and relaxed?

**GRANDPA** Well, I don't see why you just can't agree with me. History at one time involved everybody. Good and bad. There was more than one discussion or interpretation. But now it's—

**COURTNEY** *(Exploding.)* Are you living in a cave?? I haven't changed my mind about this! The history being taught today is the same *everywhere*!

**GRANDPA** How do you know that?

**COURTNEY** It's the history told through the eyes of dead white men! That's part of why I'm getting my PhD! To represent a different voice!

**GRANDPA** You sound like those pansy-asses in the state legislature. Trying to re-write the textbooks

for our schools! Saying that the world has always
been ruled by power-hungry, racist white men.

**COURTNEY**  It has.

**GRANDPA**  Oh, I forgot. That's your whole *theme*.
White males are to blame for everything. Liberal
horse manure! I didn't think my granddaughter was
*this* extreme!

**COURTNEY**  *Extreme?* Grandpa, a minute ago
you were making fun of black people! What would
you call *that*?

**GRANDPA**  I said they didn't get *married*. I didn't
make fun of them!

**COURTNEY**  Is there a difference? I'm writing my
dissertation on African Americans—African
American pilots, that is—so I happen to find what
you say offensive.

**GRANDPA**  Well, I happen to have *served* with
black Americans. So I know a thing or two about
'em myself.

**COURTNEY** You know a thing or two about *what*? The way you *chose* to remember them?

**GRANDPA** I know a thing or two about their behavior, period.

**COURTNEY** Oh, please. Whatever. This is pointless.

> *(Pause. She stops working and looks at her phone.)*

**GRANDPA** It is not pointless.

**COURTNEY** If you say so. *(Reading her phone.)* Shit. This is getting crazy. Fifty-five miles an hour.

**GRANDPA** Huh?

**COURTNEY** There's a newsflash on my phone. The winds are already at fifty-five miles an hour. Out at the airport.

**GRANDPA** Wow . . .

**COURTNEY** Ugghh. My reception is just about gone.

*(Pause. She toys with the phone, then gradually resumes working.)*

**GRANDPA**  So . . . the Tuskegee airmen, huh?

**COURTNEY**  I'd rather drop all of this, Grandpa. But, yes. The Tuskegee airmen.

**GRANDPA**  Fine pilots.

**COURTNEY**  Of course they were. They were damned fine pilots.

**GRANDPA**  Those poor bastards had to put up with a lot. But they were decent pilots. How long is your dissertation?

**COURTNEY**  It's, uh, it's right around 90 pages. It's actually here somewhere. *(Beat. She stops and looks around, confused.)* It's on my jump drive. Shit. I have *got* to find that. I don't know where I put ANYTHING! I had it earlier, right in this room! *(Beat.)* Grandpa, I can't talk. I've got to finish these windows! *(Continues working.)*

**GRANDPA**  Sheesh, I wish I could help. Why in hell are ya'll covering both sides of the windows?

**COURTNEY**  Because some of the wood around the outside widows is cracked and old.

**GRANDPA**  Cracked?

**COURTNEY**  Just in some areas. It's hard to screw in plywood cleanly over the windows. The clapboard is all bumpy and uneven.

**GRANDPA**  These old nineteenth-century clapboard houses. I don't why your parents ever bought this place.

**COURTNEY**  Shai and Joel need to hurry up! I need their help.
    *(Pause.)*
Do you think they both went to your house?

**GRANDPA**  Hell if I know. But your uncle is the *last* person I want in my house.

**COURTNEY**  I don't know how we're going to be able to communicate with anybody *(Stops and looks at her phone again. She pushes buttons, over and over, and finally puts phone down on the table.)*

**GRANDPA**  What are you doing?

**COURTNEY** That's it. We have no reception. None!

**GRANDPA** You act like you've never been through a tropical storm before.

**COURTNEY** Huh?

**GRANDPA** You know what happens. The storm will come though. The power will be out for a while. And we'll just wait. The storm will blow over like it always does.
> *(Pause as he stares at her.)*
Right?

**COURTNEY** I . . . I hope so. *(She resumes working.)*

**GRANDPA** Anyway . . . funny. You just said 'fifty-five miles an hour.' That was actually one of the levels of takeoff speed for the American pilots. I used to hear that number a lot from some of those guys down at the senior center. Some of the pilots that were from Galveston. They used to brag like hell.

**COURTNEY**  Damn! We're going to need a lot more batteries for these drills!

**GRANDPA**  Honey, those German sons of bitches were ferocious. They were something else. I'll tell you what. The Tuskegee airmen were a fine bunch but they couldn't hold a candle to the German Air Force. *(Beat. She stops and looks at him.)*

**COURTNEY**  What . . . what did you mean earlier? You made some *calls*?

**GRANDPA**  Wha . . ? No, I was just talking about the Germans and the—

**COURTNEY**  You said you made some calls. To whom?

**GRANDPA**  Oh, that. Yeah. A few months ago I made some calls for you. I knew you were looking for work. So I called some people I used to work with.

**COURTNEY**  *Who*, Grandpa?

**GRANDPA**  Well, the University of Texas, for one. I know a guy there.

**COURTNEY** *(Incredulous.)* I just can't believe this.

**GRANDPA** I also called North Texas, up in Denton. My second cousin works up there in admissions. At least he used to. I don't think you ever knew him.

**COURTNEY** *(Stunned at what she's hearing.)* This is not happening. I can't do this now . . .

**GRANDPA** Well, you don't sound very grateful. I don't know what it can lead to. But it's a start.

**COURTNEY** Do me a favor . . . AND DON'T CALL ANYBODY!

**GRANDPA** That's gratitude for you!!

**COURTNEY** Grandpa, it doesn't WORK that way!! You were never a professor. Just a high school teacher! You don't just call up a university and refer your granddaughter for a teaching job!

**GRANDPA** Why not??

**COURTNEY** There's no time for this! I don't even know why Shai had to go and get you! *(Resuming her work.)* First, all your blabbering about the Palestinians, and then African Americans, and, and the German's *so-called* superiority, and then—

**GRANDPA** They *were* superior! The Germans had better training!

**COURTNEY** Keep your opinions to yourself! There's a crisis to deal with here!

**GRANDPA** These ain't opinions! I was there. I saw them! What the hell's Ruby been teaching you?

**COURTNEY** Ruby didn't teach me anything. She never did.

**GRANDPA** Someone in this family did.

**COURTNEY** *Family*? Hah. There *is* no *family* in this family.

**GRANDPA** Yes there is.

**COURTNEY** No there's not. You sound like Shai and his stupid ideals of *family*. You said so yourself:

everybody just goes and does their own thing. Like Dad. Like you. Like Mom, taking off to the Middle East.

**GRANDPA**  Well. What does her leaving say about *you?*

**COURTNEY**  *Me*? Grandpa, what does it say about *you?* *(Beat. Explodes with sudden paranoia)* Oh my God, what am I DOING?? Why am I arguing with you?? I have *got* to find my jump drive! My DISSERTATION!!

> *(Pause as she starts ripping through drawers, through boxes and bags, looking everywhere. There is the sound of more banging from outside that gradually increases over the next minute. Here, GRANDPA should roll his chair around while talking, and wind up far stage left or right.)*

**GRANDPA**  Well . . . if it's that thing on how good the Tuskegee pilots were, then you can throw it away. I told you, they *were* good. But compared to the—

**COURTNEY** Would you shut the hell up?? This is exactly why I want to teach at a university. To shut up people like you!!

**GRANDPA** Can you hear yourself? You act like you don't come from a white family!

**COURTNEY** There's no time, Grandpa. No time to prove how wrong you are.

**GRANDPA** How do you know I'm wrong?? I was in Germany in 1945! I've seen things! I've seen things that'll make your skin crawl, girl!

**COURTNEY** Please . . .

**GRANDPA** And I told you, you might not even need that dissertation! I'm trying to help you get a job! I made those phone calls for you!

**COURTNEY** You're just gonna wind up hurting me!!

**GRANDPA** I'm trying to *help* you! I've been trying to tell you that all along! *(Beat. He sticks his head slightly offstage, and looks out.)* That banging wood out there is driving me bananas! Can I help fix that? Jesus . . .

**COURTNEY** No, you cannot.

**GRANDPA** It's out here, on the porch. Is there a drill handy? *(Enter JOEL, who walks right out in front of GRANDPA, surprising him. He is holding his hammer.)*

**GRANDPA** Aghhh! I thought you left!!

**JOEL** Calm down, Gramps.

**COURTNEY** Joel? What happened? Why are you out there?

**JOEL** I'm working out here.

**GRANDPA** I told you he was a lunatic!! I told you about him!

**COURTNEY** Grandpa, quit! *(Lights go to black for a few seconds.)*

**GRANDPA** Wha . . ?? Agghhh!!

**COURTNEY** Oh God, the power! Not now!!
>  *(The lights come back on.)*

That's it! The power is going out! Joel, where is Shai?

**GRANDPA** Keep him away from me!

**JOEL** You've got a big mouth, old man. *(Lights go out again. Stage is completely black.)*

**COURTNEY** Oh no! Joel!! Grandpa!

**GRANDPA** Hey! Where is he? HEY!!! COURTNEY! COURTNEY!!!!

>  *(Silence. Stage remains black. End of ACT ONE)*

# ACT TWO
## <u>Scene One</u>

At RISE: *Hours later, that evening, in one of the unused bedrooms. The room has a table and a few chairs. There are several candles, bottles of water, screws, nails, batteries, and a small radio on the table. A few large boxes are strewn throughout the room. The wind is quiet at the beginning but gradually picks up louder and louder throughout this act. GRANDPA coughs throughout all of ACT TWO, starting very lightly at first. SHAI is slowly lighting candles as the scene opens.*

**SHAI** How many fingers? *Three?*

**GRANDPA** Yep. He lost three fingers. Or most of three fingers.

**SHAI** Wow. I was pretty small the last time that I saw him. So I don't remember looking at his hand.

**GRANDPA** Why do you think he's wearing those gloves?

**SHAI** Yeah. Hmmm.

**GRANDPA**  He probably always wears them. Probably ashamed of his hand.

**SHAI**  Hmm.

**GRANDPA**  Anyway . . . when it happened, I don't know what the hell either of us were thinking. Me, I just stood there and watched Joel do it.

**SHAI**  You watched him do it?

**GRANDPA**  Well . . . sort of. Neither one of us thought the blades were that close to the lawnmower frame. But something was making a helluva racket. You know, on the inside, around the edge of the frame. I wished we had just turned the damned motor off. But we didn't. So I told Joel to just stick his fingers around the inside edge, try to find whatever it was making that noise.

**SHAI**  Wait. You *told* him to?

**GRANDPA**  Well, yeah. I didn't think he would actually stick his fingers in there. But yeah. I told him to. And that's about when he started screaming.

**SHAI**  Oh no . . .

**GRANDPA** And the blood . . . Lord, the blood was everywhere. It was like a busted water main. Just everywhere.

**SHAI** Oh man.

**GRANDPA** All over the green grass, over the antbeds. It was ol Dorothy Remick's yard, and she must have had a million antbeds in that grass. Blood was everywhere. All over the lawnmower engine. I never was able to clean every bit of that blood off that damn mower. Anyway, your uncle, well, he was screaming and yelling. And then your dad drove up and jumped out, and started screaming at me.

**SHAI** God.

**GRANDPA.** *God* is right. All your father seemed to care about was your uncle. They jumped in that car and peeled outta there, for the hospital. And I was left there alone, staring at all that blood.

    *(Pause.)*

I only saw your uncle a few times after that. He threatened me.

**SHAI** Did he?

**GRANDPA** Yes. And he meant it. So that's why I don't want anything to do with him.

**SHAI** But Grandpa . . . he's family. He's my uncle.

> *(Enter COURTNEY, holding a flashlight, distressed. She spends the next few minutes frantically looking through the room's boxes and bags for her zip drive.)*

**GRANDPA** They didn't seem to care that *I* was family too! Maybe I wanted to go to the hospital with them! I mean, I don't know . . .

**SHAI** Well.
> *(Pause.)*
Any luck, Courtney?

**COURTNEY** Nope. I can hardly see anything in there. This flashlight is nearly dead.

**GRANDPA** Did you find my box?

**COURTNEY** No! I don't have time to look for your dumb box!

**GRANDPA** Ughhh!

**SHAI** Where is uncle Joel?

**COURTNEY** He's in the den. Or somewhere. He helped me hang the last few tablecloths over the kitchen window.

**SHAI** Good.

**COURTNEY** But then he walked off.

**GRANDPA** What's he doing?

**COURTNEY** I don't know what he's doing.

**GRANDPA** Well, let him stay in there.

**SHAI** Is it worse in the kitchen? Is there more rain coming in?

**COURTNEY** It's not good, Shai. There's water everywhere, and broken glass. It's a wreck in there.

**SHAI** The only damned kitchen window that wasn't protected!

**COURTNEY** Tell me about it. And there's nothing left to cover it up. We don't have any tarps or anything. We need to stay in this room since there aren't any windows in here. *(Resumes looking.)* I can't believe this.

**SHAI**  Courtney, I've already gone through those boxes.

**COURTNEY**  Are you sure??

**SHAI**  Yes. I didn't see it.

**COURTNEY**  I just want to be positive. It's tiny. You may have missed it.

**SHAI**  You didn't back that thing up at all? Anywhere else?

**COURTNEY**  No.

**SHAI**  There's only one copy??

**COURTNEY**  I don't trust people at the university, Shai. You know that. It's *my* work.

**SHAI**  Suit yourself. *(Turning back to GRANDPA)* That's a crazy story, Grandpa. Mom once told us that what happened between ya'll was tragic. But I never did ask her about the details.

**GRANDPA** Tragic. Yep. *(Beat.)* Hmmph. What else did Ruby say was *tragic*?

**SHAI** Huh?

**GRANDPA** She didn't tell you other things about me that were *tragic*? I mean, with Ruby, you never know.

**COURTNEY** What have you two been talking about? Grandpa, what are you trying to say?

**GRANDPA** Do you not listen? What else has your mother said about me??

**COURTNEY** Mom hasn't told us *anything*! Tragic or otherwise! Grandpa, let's face it: we hardly know you! That's the problem: nobody knows anything about anybody!

**SHAI** Here we go . . .

**GRANDPA**  Well, calm down. I've just always wondered what she's told ya'll about me over the years. That's all. We haven't always communicated.

**COURTNEY**  *(Bristling.)* That's being generous . . .

**GRANDPA**  Hell, ya'll grew up. Moved around the country, here and there. I didn't even know that Shai had gotten married until after he divorced.

**SHAI**  Separated.

**GRANDPA**  Well, *separated*, then. I didn't even know you'd married a . . a . . .

**COURTNEY**  Go on. Say it.

**GRANDPA**  Well, a *witch,* right?

**SHAI**  She's not a witch, Grandpa.

**GRANDPA**  That's the impression I'm getting.

**SHAI**  She's a Wiccan. Not a *witch.* You would like her. You would like my son, too.

**GRANDPA**  Your . . . oh, your *son*?

**SHAI**  Yes. My son. You would like them both.

**COURTNEY**  Stop, Shai. It's not your actual *son*.

**GRANDPA**  That's what I don't understand. Why do you call him your son?

**SHAI**  He's just . . . well, he's . . .

**COURTNEY**  He's Vicki's son.

**SHAI**  *(Very flustered)* Just never mind! He's not my *actual* son. I *call* him my son. That's all!

**GRANDPA**  Well . . . all of this is just what I'm talking about. I just don't get how generations can break down over time. But it happens. This family is just . . . just so withered.

**COURTNEY**  Withered??

**GRANDPA**  You heard me. Withered. Withered away. Look at Ruby. Gone. Look at your psychotic uncle. Where's he been the last nine years? Out in the desert or some such?

**COURTNEY**  Why don't you go and ask him?

**GRANDPA**  I'll pass. And speaking of him, I don't need him jumping out at me like that again.

**SHAI**  Grandpa, relax. He wasn't trying to scare you earlier. He just stayed behind to work on the outside windows. We told you that.

**GRANDPA**  Well. I hope that's true.

**SHAI**  It is. We told you.

**GRANDPA**  Anyway. Yeah. *Withered* is the word. Look at you two. No children.

**COURTNEY**  Excuse me??

**GRANDPA**  Think about it. Are your liberal ambitions really more important than the value of family?

**COURTNEY**  Whatever.

**GRANDPA**  But seriously. Are they?

**COURTNEY** My ambition is to become a history professor. Something you may have ruined because of the *calls* you made!

**GRANDPA** But look . . . here we go again: what *kind* of history? More of that revisionist horse manure?

**COURTNEY** What??

**GRANDPA** Revisionist history. For example, earlier, you were all gung-ho over the Palestinians. So I suppose now you're going to tell me that those radical bastards weren't hijacking our planes long *before* 9/11?
>        *(Pause.)*
And then I guess you're going to keep telling me how the Tuskegee pilots outranked the Germans?

**COURTNEY** I'm about to tell you to go to hell.

**GRANDPA** You sound just like your mother. Always angry. Ruby, God, she was always ticked at something.

**COURTNEY** Would you stop??

**GRANDPA**  Mad at how "racist and unfair" everything is. Always angry at Columbus or Washington or some other white male. Always siding with the Arabs. Always knocking the Jews. I don't know how Ruby sleeps at night. She's so liberal I'm surprised she's even able to function.
*(Pause.)*
I hope you don't become like that.

**COURTNEY**  I am not just some *liberal!* I'm a *historian*! Someone who's career you have may jilted!
*(Pause.)*
What am I doing? This is pointless. I've got to find my zip drive. *(Kicks a box, begins to storm out.)*

**GRANDPA**  And I've got to find my missing box! My important papers!

**SHAI**  Courtney, you shouldn't be in that part of the house! You said so yourself!

**COURTNEY**  Watch me!!

**GRANDPA**  Could you please look for my things??

**COURTNEY**  Why the hell should I?

**GRANDPA**  Because I'm your grandfather, that's why!

**COURTNEY**  Sorry but that's not a good enough reason. *(She exits in a hurry. GRANDPA bangs his hands on the arm of wheelchair.)*

**GRANDPA**  Damnation! What's wrong with that girl?

**SHAI**  Grandpa, I'm sure the box is fine. It's in there somewhere.

**GRANDPA**  I need it. I don't like that *Joel* can get to it!

**SHAI**  It'll be fine, Grandpa.

**GRANDPA**  It's important! If it were *your* social security papers or journals, *you'd* be concerned. If it were a bunch of *comic books*, I'm sure you'd be even more concerned! We should have just stayed in the living room.

**SHAI**  Huh?? *You* saw all that water and wind coming through that window! (Stands up to exit.) Look, I'll go look for it. Be right back.

**GRANDPA**  No!

**SHAI**  No what?

**GRANDPA**  No. Just stay here. Please.

**SHAI**  I'll just go and look for it. I'll be right back.

**GRANDPA**  No! *(Coughs)* Shai, stay right here. Please. I don't want to be alone. Please.

**SHAI**  Well. Okay.

**GRANDPA**  I don't want to chance Joel coming in here without you or Courtney around.

**SHAI**  *(Sitting down.)* That box is fine. It's either in the dining room, or on that little table by the hallway. Has to be.

**GRANDPA**  Dammit. I don't know why we didn't just bring it back here.

**SHAI**  You know why. The power went out. A tree limb smashed that window. You were terrified of uncle Joel. So—

**GRANDPA** I know, I know. Dammit.

> *(Pause. He coughs again, and gradually does so throughout the rest of the scene.)*

**SHAI** Grandpa, I'm so sorry I couldn't get your medicine. Ughhhh.

**GRANDPA** Can't do anything about it now, sonny. I'll be okay.

**SHAI** I should have driven right past that stupid cop. I never dreamed there'd be a roadblock during a storm. Shoot. *(He turns on radio, gradually turns channels. Nothing but constant static.)*

**GRANDPA** Well. Maybe we'll file a lawsuit against the Galveston PD. "Old man dies because local police stopped grandson from driving across town."

**SHAI** Hmmph. Maybe . . .
> *(Pause as he listens to the static.)*
Listen to this. Nothing. Nothing at all. Unbelievable.
> *(He switches it off and quickly sifts through the bag of batteries on the table.)*

And none of these flashlight and drill batteries fit. They're the wrong size. All of them.

**GRANDPA**  No extras? Anywhere??

**SHAI**  Nope. I looked everywhere. This is it.

**GRANDPA**  What the hell are we gonna do?

**SHAI**  Pray that the flashlight lasts all night.

**GRANDPA**  Jesus . . .

**SHAI**  Indeed.
>           *(Pause. He stares at phone, shakes his head in frustration.)*

God . . . I hope they're okay.

**GRANDPA**  Oh. Your . . . family?

**SHAI**  Yes. They should be here with us. If something happened to my son . . . Grandpa, if something happened to him, I'm scared to think of what I might do.
>           *(Pause.)*

I really am. *(Beat.)* You . . . were talking about our family being withered.

**GRANDPA** Yeah.

**SHAI** I didn't like it at first.

**GRANDPA** Oh?

**SHAI** But now I wonder if you might be right. Vicki's mom is always telling me and Vicki that our generation isn't having enough children. That we're selfish. That everything is about *us*. Generation X, she calls us.

**GRANDPA** Gen X. I've heard that term before.

**SHAI** Yeah. *(Points at himself.)* That's us. Me and Courtney.
        *(Pause. He is in deep thought.)*
But it makes me sick, Grandpa.

**GRANDPA** What makes you sick?

**SHAI** My generation. Courtney. Myself. Vicki. My friends. All of us. It's true. Most of us *aren't* having kids. We *are* selfish. We do what we want.
        *(Pause.)*
And maybe we make this family more withered than it already is.

**GRANDPA**  Mmmm.

> *(Pause. He coughs, and is increasingly uncomfortable.)*

I don't know.

**SHAI**  That's why I care so much. I'd like to make a difference in this family. Bring it together. Or at least, try to.

**GRANDPA**  Shai?

**SHAI**  Yeah?

**GRANDPA**  Sorry. I . . . I really want my box. It's very personal to me.

**SHAI**  I told you I can go look for it.

**GRANDPA**  Well. Maybe you should, after all. Do you mind?

> *(A very loud thump is heard from within the house)*

**SHAI**  Whoa!

**GRANDPA**  What in the hell was that?

**SHAI**  I don't know!

**GRANDPA**  It was just down the hallway! Towards the kitchen! Damnation!

**SHAI**  I think a tree just fell on the roof!

**GRANDPA**  That *was* a tree! It had to have been!

*(Enter COURTNEY, wet, out of breath.)*

**SHAI**  Courtney, what happened??

**COURTNEY**  Oh my God! A gigantic tree limb came right through the living room ceiling! I was standing right there!

**SHAI**  Are you okay??

**COURTNEY**  I'm fine, yes. *(Breathing heavily, trying to calm down)* I'm okay. There was rain, and wind, and everything. It all came crashing down at once!

**GRANDPA**  Jesus . . . it didn't fall though in the kitchen, did it?

**SHAI** Where's Uncle Joel?

**COURTNEY** I don't know! Oh, shit, Shai, that limb is huge! It kept sliding down!

**GRANDPA** So where is Joel??

**COURTNEY** He's still in there! In the den! He had a lantern, and he was in there, muttering to himself about something.

**SHAI** He had a *what?*

**COURTNEY** I think he went out and got one of those old lanterns from the garage. *(Sits down, gradually calms down)* I don't know what he was doing. I was so busy looking for my jump drive. He kept talking to himself, looking at something. Reading something, I think. Oh Shai, there's water all over the living room and kitchen!

**SHAI** We're okay in here. I don't think there are any limbs over this part of the house.

**COURTNEY** What about all those oak trees by the back bedrooms?? Isn't that right over us? *(Points upwards, at the ceiling.)*

**SHAI** *(Realizing their exact location.)* Oh . . . *those*
. . . yeah.

**GRANDPA** Did you find my journals? My box?

**COURTNEY** I didn't look for your damn box! I
was looking for my own stuff!

**GRANDPA** Dammit, girl!

**COURTNEY** Grandpa, YOU aren't the only one
here needing something!
   *(Pause.)*
Shai, listen. I'm panicking. I need you to think
really hard. Are you *sure* you didn't move my jump
drive? Or put it somewhere?

**SHAI** I remember seeing it, on the kitchen table.
But I promise I didn't move it.

**COURTNEY** I'm starting to get hysterical!

**GRANDPA** I need my box!

**COURTNEY** And *I* need my thesis!

**SHAI** Can you guys please STOP???

**GRANDPA**  I just can't understand why you couldn't look around for it. It was in the kitchen. You had to have seen it!

**COURTNEY**  Grandpa . . . I WAS LOOKING FOR MY JUMP DRIVE. Do you know how many thousands of hours of work there are on that drive?? That work is my life!

**GRANDPA**  But I've already told you! You should just start over!

**SHAI**  Grandpa, stop! I'll go and get your box!

**GRANDPA**  No! She needs to hear this!

**COURTNEY**  I swear if you weren't my grandfather, I'd—I don't know WHAT I'd do!

**GRANDPA**  What a way to respect your elders.

> *(She steps back and kicks a chair hard. Then, another loud thump is heard from above. Everybody is jolted; they look upward)*

**COURTNEY** What the hell?

**GRANDPA** That's right above us!

**SHAI** Dang, that *is* above us!

> *(Enter JOEL, behind GRANDPA, unseen. He is carrying an old lantern and a fist full of papers. He is very wet.)*

**COURTNEY** Shit! What do we do?? *(Sees him.)* Joel!

**GRANDPA** AAYYY!! Get him away from me!

**JOEL** These your books, Pops?

**SHAI** Guys, let's move! We need to get out of here!

> *(SHAI starts to maneuver the wheelchair out of the room. COURTNEY begins to exit. GRANDPA grabs drill off the table for protection.)*

**JOEL** These belong to you? Huh?? *(He holds the papers out, as if on display.)*

**GRANDPA**  Give me that!!

**COURTNEY**  Joel, the ceiling is going to collapse!
Come on!

**SHAI**  Let's go!!

**JOEL**  Finders, keepers, Gramps.

**GRANDPA**  I WANT THOSE PAPERS, YOU
JUVENILE!!

**JOEL**  What are you going to do?? Cut off another
finger to get them back??

**GRANDPA**  I'LL KILL YOU!!!

> *(As they exit in a mad rage, the lights fade to
> black. The wind continues to whistle, very
> loudly. End of scene.)*

# ACT TWO
## <u>Scene Two</u>

At RISE: *A bedroom down the hall, just a few minutes later. Like the previous room, it is outdated and unused. There are a few random boxes on the floor and a small table. When the lights go up, everybody except JOEL is rushing into the room.*

**SHAI** Okay! Grandpa, we should be safe in here.

**GRANDPA** Where is that maniac?? Did he run off again?

**SHAI** He didn't follow us. I don't know.

**COURTNEY** I can't believe this! We never finished the windows back here.

**SHAI** I didn't think we needed to!

**COURTNEY** What??

**SHAI** I didn't think we'd ever come back here for shelter!

**COURTNEY** Come on, let's get started! They're all exposed!! The outside wasn't done either!

**SHAI** I have plenty of screws. *(Pulling screws from his pocket.)*

**SHAI** There's plywood in here, thank God. Where is the drill?

**COURTNEY** It's in the other room!

**GRANDPA** No . . . here it is.

> *(He hands drill to SHAI. He is exhausted with emotion, and gradually speaks slower and slower. For the next several minutes SHAI drills wood over the windows while COURTNEY shines the light on his work.)*

**SHAI** Oh, good. Great. *(Takes drill.)* Courtney, you hold the light. I'll work the drill.

**COURTNEY** Okay.

**GRANDPA** Are we . . . gonna be okay in here?

**SHAI** We'll do what we can, Grandpa.

**GRANDPA** Where is Joel? He had my journals . . . my papers.

**SHAI** He didn't follow us in here, Grandpa.

**GRANDPA** Why does he keep disappearing??

**COURTNEY** What are you worried about, Grandpa? Huh? What did Joel find in your precious papers?

**GRANDPA** I don't know . . .

**COURTNEY** What was it? Huh?

**SHAI** Courtney, keep the light steady!

**COURTNEY** I am.

**GRANDPA** Ohhhh . . *(From here forward, GRANDPA gradually moans, more and more, greatly distressed, is near-delusional, etc.)*

**COURTNEY** What did Joel find? Tell me, dear grandfather.

**SHAI** Courtney, you keep moving the flashlight! And these screws keep slipping too!

**COURTNEY** No, it's the drill. It's going dead.

**SHAI** And we have no extra batteries! Aghhh!

**GRANDPA** Ohhhhh . . .

**COURTNEY** What were you so worried about, Grandpa? Huh?

**SHAI** Courtney, stop!

**COURTNEY** No! He may have ruined my teaching career so I don't mind ruining his life. Or what's left of it, anyway. Was it *Mom*, Grandpa? What did you do to Mom?

**GRANDPA** I love your mother. I've always loved her.

**COURTNEY** Then what were you worried about? Tell me! *(She flashes the light across the room, into his face)*

**GRANDPA** *(Shielding his face with his hands.)*
Aghhhh!

**SHAI** Courtney!! The LIGHT!

**COURTNEY** *(Turning light back to the work.)* It's
almost dead, Shai. It's getting weaker and weaker.

**SHAI** Leave Grandpa alone! *(Bangs drill against
wall in frustration)*
Come on, we need each other here!!

**COURTNEY** No! I want to know. It's bad enough
that he's our own grandfather and we hardly know
him!! *(Beat. SHAI stops working and looks at her.)*

**SHAI** Where did Joel go?

**COURTNEY** I don't know.

**SHAI** *(Calling out.)* JOEL! HEY, UNCLE JOEL!

**GRANDPA** I need my box . . . I want those
papers . . .

**COURTNEY** If I can't find my jump drive, then
you can't get your stupid papers!!

**SHAI** Courtney, come on, back to work! *(They gradually resume working. COURTNEY is fixated on GRANDPA.)*

**COURTNEY** Remember my high school boyfriend? You used to grumble about *him. He* was African American, and you didn't like it! And now you come to our house, babbling your conservative crap. Criticizing my career! You made those stupid phone calls! Well, the women of my generation are breaking the barriers down, old man!

**SHAI** Why is *that* important now?? Why are you doing this?

**COURTNEY** He's using us, Shai. He's only here because of the hurricane. *He's* the reason we didn't finish the windows!! *He's* the reason I lost my jump drive!! Do you know how far that's going to set me back? In getting my PhD?

**SHAI** It's your own fault you didn't back your work up.

**COURTNEY** Bringing him here was a mistake!

**SHAI** No it wasn't.

**COURTNEY**  He's just riding the storm out, and then he's out of here!! What kind of *grandfather* is that?

**SHAI**  Courtney, the wind is getting stronger. *(Putting his head against the wall, listening to the storm.)* I can feel it through this wall. Shit.

**GRANDPA**  *(Slowly reflecting.)* That night . . . ohh, that night was exactly like this.

**SHAI**  Grandpa, are you okay? We're gonna be fine. Just hang on!

**GRANDPA**  Everything was wet and muddy . . . it was dark.

**COURTNEY**  The very name 'grandfather' is an insult. He's never been there for us!! He called people, Shai! He called people at the universities where I've applied to teach. Do you know how bad that looks?? How *unprofessional*? He inhibited Mom's career too!

**SHAI**  He did not!

**COURTNEY** She could have been a fine professor! He didn't encourage her either!!

**SHAI** He's your grandfather!! Show some respect!!

**COURTNEY** What kind of grandfather makes phone calls without first asking her? Is that *family*? What kind of Grandpa belittles his granddaughter's ambitions?!

**SHAI** What kind of granddaughter uses such hateful language??

**COURTNEY** I want to know what he was worried about!! With those papers!

**GRANDPA** Ohhh . . .

**SHAI** Courtney, how do you know there was *anything* to those papers? They're just Grandpa's old journals. Maybe Joel was just talking nonsense!! *(Beat. He takes a big breath, stops working, is very weary)* Oh, I . . . I can't do this . . . I can't . . .

> *(There is another very loud thump, followed by more blasts of wind and breaking glass.*

*GRANDPA covers his eyes and moans, is*
*even more delusional.)*

**COURTNEY** That's another tree limb!!

**SHAI** How many more are going to fall?? How
many?

**COURTNEY** Come on, keep working!!

**SHAI** We should have evacuated! *(Begins to bang*
*the drill against the wall in anger.)* We should have
left Galveston!! Why are we still here??

**COURTNEY** Shai, snap out of it!

**SHAI** *(Continuing to hit the wall with the drill.)*
This old house! This stupid old house! This
ridiculous family!!

**COURTNEY** Don't you lose it too, Shai!

**SHAI** Where is Vicki? Where is MY SON?? Damn
this storm . . . Damn THADDEUS!!
DAMN THIS FAMILY!! DAMN VICKI AND
HER STUPID WICCA BULLSHIT!!

**COURTNEY** Shai!!

**SHAI** MOM'S IN PALESTINE!! DAD'S OUT IN THE DESERT! THIS IS NO FAMILY!!

**COURTNEY** Shai, keep it TOGETHER!

**SHAI** This is no family, Courtney. Ohhhhhh . . . *(Crying)* Why . . . why did we stay in Galveston? *(He hits the wall slower now)* Why are we here!?

**COURTNEY** Shai! You are sounding like Grandpa! Come on, get it together!

**SHAI** But it's true!! And what do you care?? All you care about is your teaching ambitions! About becoming a college professor!!

**COURTNEY** Shai!!

**SHAI** IT'S ALL TRUE!!

**COURTNEY** I DO CARE, SHAI!! I DO!

**SHAI** *How* do you care??

**COURTNEY** I care about us! We have each other! Right here! *You and me!!*

*(Pause. He stares at her, stunned.)*

**COURTNEY** *That* is family! Right there! You and I. No matter how small it seems. It's something. I *do* care. I care about that. *(Beat. They continue to look at each other, breathing heavy.)* We've got each other, Shai. And . . . *that's* family.

> *(Long pause. COURTNEY grabs the drill and light, resumes working. SHAI collects himself.)*

**COURTNEY** And I don't want you to ever forget that.

**GRANDPA** It was just like this . . . when we caught them.

**SHAI** Grandpa . . . we're going to make it. Okay? Grandpa, you hang in there.

**GRANDPA** We caught them . . .

**COURTNEY** What are you saying?? *(Another loud thump is heard from above.)*

**COURTNEY** That's another limb on the roof!

**SHAI** Oh God! Where is Joel?

**COURTNEY** I think it's right there in the hallway!

**SHAI** *(Calling out)* Uncle Joel!! Uncle!!

**COURTNEY** Shai, come on. *(Passing him the flashlight.)* Hold the light! We've gotta cover these windows!

**SHAI** Are we gonna stay in this room?

**COURTNEY** We may have to! We may be trapped in here!

**GRANDPA** I can't take this . . . so much noise . . .

**SHAI** Grandpa, it's going to be okay.

**GRANDPA** Ohhhh . . . Shai . . .

**SHAI** It's going to be fine.

**COURTNEY** *(As she works with the drill.)* I'm still not finished with you, Grandpa.

**SHAI** *(Calling out again.)* Uncle Joel! Uncle!? *(Beat as he looks out into the hallway.)*

Oh God, Courtney, you were right. There's water coming right down through the hallway ceiling!!

**COURTNEY**  You weren't so quiet earlier, old man! Criticizing me! Making fun of my desire to teach!!

**GRANDPA**  Ohhh . . .

**SHAI**  Courtney, there's a gigantic pine limb there in the hallway! Right through the ceiling! We can't leave this room!

**COURTNEY**  I WANT TO KNOW WHAT GRANDPA WAS WORRIED ABOUT!! *(Slamming the drill against the wall.)*

**GRANDPA**  Stop . . . please.

**SHAI**  *(Grabbing her arm)* You'd better chill, right now! *You're* the one that was just talking about family!! Weren't you?? *(Pointing at the hallway.)* And we've got a real problem. Right out there!!

**COURTNEY**  I know all about it. I can see it too!!

*(She shrugs him off and keeps working. SHAI turns and kneels at GRANDPA's chair.)*

**SHAI**  Grandpa, this storm will soon pass, okay? We can take you back home. You can take your medicine.

**GRANDPA**  I wish you could have been there, Shai. It was dark. So dark.

**SHAI**  Grandpa, it's going to be fine! We'll have dinner when this is all over with! Maybe you can meet my son!!

**GRANDPA**  They were up in the loft. And when we caught them . . .we didn't know what to do.

**SHAI**  Who . . .??

**GRANDPA**  But . . . we were so angry. They were traitors . . .

**SHAI**  Grandpa, *who?* What are you talking about?

**COURTNEY**  He's lost it, Shai.

**GRANDPA** The rain was coming down so hard. Biblical, that's what my friend called it. A biblical storm. Oh, Shai . . .

**SHAI** Grandpa, we'll have your medicine for you in the morning! It'll be fine!

> *(There is another loud thump from above, though not as loud.)*

**COURTNEY** Oh God!

**SHAI** Aghhh!

**COURTNEY** That's right above us, Shai!! We need to get outta this room!

**SHAI** Where to?? We can't move grandpa down that hallway!

**COURTNEY** Oh, damn . . . damn . . .

> *(GRANDPA is moaning louder than ever. He puts his head down, props it up with his hands.)*

**GRANDPA**  Ohhhh . . . it was terrible. I was in the 97th Infantry, and I was so proud of it. And it was a beautiful night.

**SHAI**  Grandpa, stop!

**GRANDPA**  But then there was the blood . . .

**COURTNEY**  Snap out of it!

**GRANDPA**  No! LISTEN!!

> *(Pause. COURTNEY and SHAI stop and just stare at him)*

**GRANDPA**  We caught them. We shot them, Shai!! The blood ran so thick and dark, all over the hay in that loft

**SHAI**  Grandpa . . ?

**GRANDPA**  We shot those black soldiers!! Our own American men!! We killed them right there in that barn! They were screwing a couple of German girls. Right there in the loft!

**SHAI**  GRANDPA!!

**GRANDPA** Two black soldiers . . . Americans! Having sex with the enemy! And we shot them!

**COURTNEY** Grandpa, don't say that . . . *(Slowly sits down, stunned, exhausted.)*

**GRANDPA** We shot them up . . . we killed them, Courtney. Those traitors! It's there, in those papers. In my journal. We shot them so many times . . . *(Moaning louder than ever)* Ohhh . . . and the dreams I have had.

**COURTNEY** The light, Shai. Turn it off. Save it.

> *(SHAI turns off flashlight. COURTNEY closes her eyes, weary and defeated. SHAI kneels by GRANDPA's chair, holding his arm, consoling him. The sounds of the outside wind accelerate and become louder until the scene ends.)*

**GRANDPA** Oh my . . . the dreams that I've had.

**COURTNEY** Oh God, help us . . .

**SHAI** Grandpa, snap out of it! It's okay, Grandpa!

**GRANDPA** The dreams . . . are just awful. I've carried this for fifty years. May God help me.

**SHAI** It's okay, Grandpa. It's going to be okay. *(He embraces him, rocks him slowly)*

**GRANDPA** I've asked for forgiveness . . . but the dreams are still there. Ohhhh . . .

**SHAI** It's all going to be okay.

> *(Long pause. The wind continues to howl, in the background. COURTNEY closes her eyes, exhausted and defeated.)*

**GRANDPA** Oh, help me, Lord. Help me . . .

**SHAI** It's going to be fine, Grandpa. Everything's fine.

> *(He repeats this several times. Lights fade to black for a few seconds. After several seconds, the lights slowly come back on. Everybody has passed out from exhaustion, sleeping. The wind still howls, though not as loud. Lights fade to black. End of scene)*

# ACT TWO
## Scene Three

At RISE: *Very early, that morning. The room is a different bedroom. JOEL and COURTNEY are working with brooms and bags, sweeping up trash and debris. There are various bags of trash everywhere, as they have been bringing the house's debris to this room. Sunlight seeps in from outside.*

**COURTNEY** How many bags do we have left, Joel?

**JOEL** Not sure. Seven. Maybe eight.

**COURTNEY** Okay. Eight bags might be enough. At least, for the mess in here.

*(Enter SHAI, holding the jump drive.)*

**JOEL** I think there are more out in the garage.

**COURTNEY** *(Notices SHAI.)* Hey.

**SHAI** So . . . looking for this??

**COURTNEY** What?? Is that it?? *(She screams in joy.)* My jump drive!! Ohhhh *(Grabbing it from him.)*

**SHAI** Thought you might like that.

**COURTNEY** Shai, where WAS it??

**SHAI** You aren't gonna believe this.

**COURTNEY** Tell me!

**SHAI** It was in Grandpa's chair!

**COURTNEY** What?

**SHAI** In that side pocket of his wheelchair! It was in there the whole time!!

**COURTNEY** WHAT?? How did it get in there??

**SHAI** Last night, when I was hanging the plywood over the windows he helped me clean a bunch of stuff off the tables. So it somehow just wound up in the side pocket of his wheelchair.

**COURTNEY** He had it the whole time??

**SHAI** We had no idea, Courtney. *He* had no idea. You know how frantic we were last night. He had all kinds of things crammed in that side pocket. Newspapers, potato chips. When I took him home he pulled everything out. And there it was. I couldn't believe it. He couldn't believe it, either.

**COURTNEY** *(Still stunned.)* Wow, wow, wow. This is crazy. Joel, can you believe it??

**JOEL** After last night . . . I don't know *what* to believe.

**SHAI** Amen to that. *(Pointing to jump drive.)* I hope that thing still works.

**COURTNEY** It looks okay. It doesn't look like it got wet or anything.

**JOEL** I'll get the rest of those bags. (Exits.)

**COURTNEY** Okay. Thanks, Joel. (Beat. She is still ecstatic.) Well . . . yeah! Ya'll don't know how happy I am!!

**SHAI** Ha. Well, we have *some* idea.

**COURTNEY**  My dissertation!!

**SHAI**  Yep. Your dissertation.

**COURTNEY**  This is . . . just fantastic! Yeah!

**SHAI**  I'm glad that you finally have it.

**COURTNEY**  So. Um . . . Shai?

**SHAI**  Yeah?

**COURTNEY**  How was Grandpa? When you left him?

**SHAI**  Well.
  *(Pause.)*
Very shaken up.

**COURTNEY**  Yeah.

**SHAI**  Might take some time to get over last night.

**COURTNEY**  Well . . . how was his house?

**SHAI**  It's actually okay. The water came up really high in the backyard. But it didn't go inside. He had two trees blown down.

**COURTNEY**  Oh. In his backyard?

**SHAI**  Yeah. But that was all.

**COURTNEY**  Are there a lot of people out driving around?

**SHAI**  There actually are.

**COURTNEY**  Wow.

**SHAI**  There are trees down everywhere. Tons of flooded areas. But people are out. On the radio they were saying the sea wall got pounded. But it made it.

**COURTNEY**  Okay. Damn.

**SHAI**  I think Grandpa's gonna be okay. He has water and some other supplies. But he'll soon need some more.

*(Enter JOEL, carrying bags.)*

**COURTNEY**  Okay.

**SHAI**  Food and other things. You know. But, yeah. He was pretty shaken up.

**JOEL**  Here you go. There are twelve bags here.

**COURTNEY** Okay, good. Twelve bags are better than eight bags, I guess.

**SHAI**  Uncle Joel, thanks for staying and helping out.

**COURTNEY**  Yeah, you've been a lot of help.

**JOEL**  Well. You're welcome.
    *(Pause.)*
I guess I'll be leaving now.

**COURTNEY**  Well. You don't have to leave.

**JOEL**  I need to see my trailer. See if it's still there.

**COURTNEY**  All right.

**SHAI**  Your car is okay? Everything good?

**JOEL**  Yes. I started it earlier. Still runs. Still in one piece.

**SHAI**  Good. That's amazing.

**JOEL**  Two windows are cracked.

**SHAI**  Oh.

**JOEL**  But it still runs.

**SHAI**  Okay.

**JOEL**  Well . . . *(Slowly turns to leave.)*

**COURTNEY**  Joel? Are we going to see you again?

**JOEL**  How's that?

**COURTNEY**  You know. Would you like to come over sometime? For a cookout or something?

**SHAI**  Yeah. You could meet my son.

**JOEL**  *(To Courtney)* I didn't think . . . that you'd be up for that.

**COURTNEY**  Huh?

**SHAI**  You *are* family, uncle Joel.

**JOEL**  *(To Courtney)* But didn't you call this family dysfunctional?

**COURTNEY**  Well . . .

**JOEL**  Last night you didn't seem excited . . . about *any* kind of family.

**COURTNEY**  No. I . . . well, last night was crazy. A lot of things were said last night. A lot of regretful things. I don't know. But . . . you're welcome to come over anytime, uncle Joel.

**JOEL**  Okay.

**COURTNEY**  Anytime.

**SHAI**  Just drop on by. No need to call.

*(Pause.)*

**JOEL**  A cookout, huh?

**COURTNEY**  That's right. A cookout.

*(Pause.)*

**JOEL**  I'd like that.
*(Pause. Turns to leave.)*
Well. I'm leaving now. Thanks for everything.

**COURTNEY**  Thank *you,* Joel.

**SHAI**  I can walk you out to your car.

**JOEL**  No. I'll leave on my own. *(Firmly.)* Alone.

**SHAI**  Oh. Okay.

**COURTNEY**  Thanks again, Joel.

**JOEL**  See ya'll sometime.

**COURTNEY**  Bye.

*(He exits. Pause.)*

**SHAI**  Wow. So. Now what?

**COURTNEY** I guess we finish cleaning everything up. That's what.

**SHAI** Yeah.

(*Beat.*)

**COURTNEY** *Are* we a dysfunctional family, Shai? What do you think?

**SHAI** Does it matter what I think? There are no perfect families. We all have an uncle Joel. Or a Grandpa. Or, ha, a Courtney or a Shai.

**COURTNEY** Yeah.

**SHAI** And we're obligated to help each other out, whenever possible. We have to extend a hand. You know. Invite them in.

**COURTNEY** But look at what happens when we invite them in. Look at last night. All that insane drama.

**SHAI** But Courtney . . . we didn't necessarily invite them here, did we?

**COURTNEY** Huh?

**SHAI** It's true. We didn't invite them. *They* came to *us*.

**COURTNEY** Oh. Well . . .

**SHAI** Right?

**COURTNEY** Yeah. I guess.

**SHAI** They needed us. Ha. We can thank Mr. Thaddeus for that. *(Musingly.)* An evening with Thaddeus.

**COURTNEY** Hmmm. An evening with Thaddeus.

> *(Pause. He turns back to the work but she stops him.)*

**COURTNEY** Hey.

**SHAI** What?

**COURTNEY** Let's go over there. To grandpa's.

**SHAI** Now?

**COURTNEY**  He needs us.

**SHAI**  Right.

**COURTNEY**  He needs things. *(Motioning to the room.)* This stuff can wait. We're young. We have each other. But he's all alone.

**SHAI**  Yeah. Okay.

**COURTNEY**  After all . . . he . . . *is* family.

**SHAI**  Yep. Let's go, then.

> *(They slowly begin to exit. COURTNEY looks around the room, attempts to take it all in with humor.)*

**COURTNEY**  Thaddeus. Ha.

**SHAI**  What a name for a hurricane.

**COURTNEY**  Thaddeus, Thaddeus . . . oh, what have you done?

**SHAI**  He's made a mess out of everyone.

**COURTNEY**  Boy. You got that right.

**SHAI**  Mm-hmm.

**COURTNEY**  You absolutely . . . got that right.

> *(They exit slowly. Lights fade to black. End of play.)*

# ☞ **About the Playwright** ☜

John Glass is a playwright and a short story writer. In 2013 he co-founded *Student Plays*, which has scripts for 5th grade through college. John has self-produced three full-length plays, and has had his plays produced in Michigan, New York, Texas, Alabama and California.

John has also published two collections of short fiction, *Pumpkins and Paint,* and *Hardball, Hi-Hats, and Haunts.* You may contact him at john@studentplays.org. Or shoot him a text at 251-463-8650.

# ☞ **More from Student Plays** ☜

## Forty Whacks

*Drama. Spooky.* **High School/College.** *25-35 minutes. 3 actors: 2 females, 1 male.*

A pair of siblings have inherited the Lizzie Borden Bed and Breakfast in New England. Although the business was run for decades in a quiet, respectable fashion, one of the siblings is over-ambitious, wanting to unearth an alleged piece of buried evidence within the house. This brings about a chilly uneasiness between brother and sister, and perhaps within the house itself.

## John Calhoun and a Thief

*Drama.* **College.** *35-40 minutes. 3 actors: 2 females, 1 male.*

Kicked out of a university PhD program, a bitter and dejected female lifts from the library archives original copies of John Calhoun's personal documents. Counseled and consoled by her roommates, her conscience slowly gets to her; but as she seeks entry to other universities her luck turns to worse, and the subsequent decisions she

124

makes regarding the historic papers cause this one-act play to become darker, if not funnier.

## Honoring the Hijacker

*Drama. **College/Adult.** 12-15 minutes. 4 actors: 2 females, 2 males.*

It's 1981, the ten-year anniversary of the famed hijacker D.B. Cooper. The play's four characters are attending a "D.B. Festival" and have stayed up very late, outlasting everybody else. The late night chit-chat goes from pranks and jokes to outright volatility, and suddenly this get-together becomes something that three of the four characters didn't bargain for.

## Harper and the Hoarder

*Drama. **Adult.** One hour. 7 actors: 5 females, 2 males.*

Long-time poet, rebel, and hoarder Faye Alexander is in desperate search of a novel given to her long ago by old friend, Harper Lee. Faye has help . . . but time is running out. The novel contains "important papers" and MUST be discovered. The clock ticks, the search goes on—amidst the piles of hoarding— and the key role of Faye's friendship with Harper Lee slowly trickles out. Gradually, everything merges to give this Southern drama an exciting climax.

## The Nonsense of Neutrons

*Drama.* **College/Adult.** *50 minutes. 5 actors: 2 f, 3 m.*

The year is 1995, and fanfare and hype over the 50th anniversary of World War Two are all around. But Shannon, a college student, is carrying a long-time rage over her family's distant connection to the war. Her friends encourage her, warily, to stay positive amidst all of the buzz. And gradually . . . the pending campus symposium of aging nuclear physicists proves pivotal to this play's climax.